SURPRISE FOR A COWBOY

By the Author

SURPRISE FOR A COWBOY

Clyde Robert Bulla

Illustrated by Grace Paull

THOMAS Y. CROWELL COMPANY
New York

To
Maude Corrinne
and Arn

Contents

SURPRISE FOR A COWBOY

What Does a Cowboy Do?

What does a cow-boy do all day?
What does a cow-boy do at night?

What does a cow-boy do all day? Rides in the pas - ture
What does a cow-boy do at night? Sleeps and dreams till

far a - way with the cat -tle on the range. Yip - pee - i - ay! —
broad day-light of the cat -tle on the range. Yip - pee - i - ay! —

Yip -pee -i - ay! ——— ay! ———
Yip -pee -i -

I

The Cowboy Game

Danny Hopper lived in the top of a big apartment house. From his window he could see the city street far below. Sometimes he saw a dog. Sometimes a fire engine went by. But most of the time there was nothing new for him to see.

He had no yard to play in. When school was

out, he had no one to play with. His mother had a cat named Jill, but Jill didn't like to play. All she did was eat and wash herself and sleep.

So Danny made up a game that he could play by himself. He called it the cowboy game.

He had a chair that he called his horse. He rode it up and down. He called his bedroom the corral and he played he was driving cattle into it. He had a piece of rope, and he could rope a calf with it. The calf was his father's footstool.

A long time ago Danny's father had been a cowboy. Now Danny wanted to be a cowboy, too.

One night Mother was reading a book. Father was reading a paper, with his feet on the footstool. Danny was riding up and down on his chair.

"Get up, pony," he said. "We'll catch that calf!"

He threw his rope. It fell over his father's feet.

"Here!" Father laughed and took the rope off his feet. "What are you doing?"

"I'm playing the cowboy game," said Danny.

"He plays it all day long," said Mother.

"I like to play cowboy." Danny sat down on the footstool by Father's chair. "Will you tell me about the ranch where you lived when you were a boy?"

"Don't you ever get tired of hearing about that?" asked Father.

"No," said Danny. "I like to hear about the ranch house and the horses and the cattle. Wasn't it fun to live on a ranch?"

"Yes," said Father. "We worked hard, but we had fun, too. My brother and I rode together and went to the roundups together. You know who my brother is, don't you?"

"He is my Uncle Mack," said Danny.

"Yes," said Father, "and now he has a big ranch of his own."

"I wish I could see a real ranch," said Danny.

Father and Mother looked at each other. Danny knew by the way they looked that they had a secret. "What is the secret?" he asked them.

"If we told it," said Mother, "it wouldn't be a secret."

"Will it be a big surprise?" asked Danny.

"Wait and see," said Father.

Danny waited. He waited a week and nothing happened.

Then one night there was a knock at the door.

Danny opened the door. A man came in. He was a tall man, and he looked a little like Father. His clothes were like the ones Father wore, but his shoes were different. The tall man wore cowboy boots.

"It's Uncle Mack!" cried Danny.

"Hello, Danny! Hello, everybody!" said Uncle Mack.

Mother and Father shook hands with him. Jill, the cat, came out of her box to see who was there. Everybody talked at once.

"I've been on the road all day," said Uncle

Mack. "Is there anything for a hungry man to eat?"

They all went into the kitchen.

"I hope you can stay a long time," said Danny.

"I can't stay long," said Uncle Mack. "I have to get back to my ranch. Are you ready to go with me?"

"Me?" Danny looked at Mother and Father. "*May* I go with Uncle Mack? May I really?"

"Do you want to go?" asked Mother.

"Yes," said Danny. "Yes, yes!"

"Good!" said Uncle Mack. "That's what I came for. I came to take you home with me for the summer."

"And this is the surprise!" said Danny.

"Do you like it?" asked Uncle Mack.

"It's the best surprise I ever had. I'm going to be a cowboy!" Danny jumped up and down. He made so much noise that Jill, the cat, laid back her ears and ran. She hid so far under the table that only her tail stuck out.

II

Bar-K Ranch

Early one morning Danny and Uncle Mack started for the ranch. When they got into the car, Danny looked out. He saw Mother and Father at their window high in the apartment house. They waved, and he waved back. Then he and Uncle Mack were on their way.

All day they rode along. They passed farms.

They crossed rivers. They stayed all night in a town.

The next day they came to the mountains.

"Are we nearly there?" asked Danny.

"Not yet," said Uncle Mack. "Look for a mountain with a flat top. When you see that, you will know we are nearly there."

Danny looked for a flat-topped mountain. He looked and looked, and after a while he almost forgot it. Then, all at once, he saw it. It was a long, low mountain with a top that looked as flat as a floor.

"I see the flat-topped mountain!" he said.

"And here is the ranch," said Uncle Mack.

They turned in at a gate. Over the gate was a sign: "Bar-K Ranch."

They drove across a pasture. At the end of a long, bumpy road, Danny saw a white house with a red roof.

A woman came out of the house.

"Here is your Aunt Betty," said Uncle Mack.
Danny called to her, "Hello, Aunt Betty!"

"Hello, Danny!" she called back. "Welcome to
Bar-K Ranch."

A collie dog came running around the house.

"Here is Shep," said Uncle Mack. "He wants
to say hello. Shake hands with Danny, Shep."

The dog barked and held out his paw. Danny
shook hands with him.

"Shep is glad to see you," said Aunt Betty, "and so am I."

Uncle Mack put the car away. Danny went into the house with Aunt Betty.

He liked the house. It was big and cool. There was one room with a deer's head on the wall. There were old guns on the wall, too, and there was a stone fireplace.

There was a room with nothing in it but chairs and a long table. "This is where the cowboys eat," Aunt Betty told him.

She showed him another room. It was small, and the walls were of pine. There was an Indian rug on the floor. By the side of the bed was a table. Under the table was a chest covered with leather. When Danny went to the window to look out, he could see the flat-topped mountain.

"I like this room best of all," he said.

"I am glad you do," said Aunt Betty. "This is your room."

Uncle Mack came in. "Have you looked in the chest?" he asked. "There is something in it for you."

Danny got down on his knees and opened the chest.

"Oh!" he said. "Here's a hat."

It was a cowboy hat. He put it on.

"See what else is in the chest," said Uncle Mack.

Danny took out a red handkerchief.

"To wear around your neck," said Aunt Betty.

He took out a blue-and-white checked shirt and a pair of blue jeans. Next he took out a pair of leather chaps. In the bottom of the chest he found a pair of fine, new cowboy boots!

Uncle Mack helped him put on his new clothes. He showed him how to put the chaps on over his jeans.

"A cowboy doesn't wear these clothes just to dress up," said Uncle Mack. "He wears a wide hat to keep off the sun and rain. He wears a handkerchief around his neck to keep out the dust."

"What are the chaps for?" asked Danny.

"Sometimes a cowboy has to ride through brush," said Uncle Mack. "When he wears chaps, the thorns can't stick him and brush can't hit him on the legs."

Danny looked at his boots. "Why does a cowboy wear boots with high heels?"

"So his feet will fit better in the stirrups when

he rides," said Uncle Mack. "I'll show you about that tomorrow."

Danny walked around in his new clothes. "Now I'm a cowboy!"

Uncle Mack laughed. "It takes more than clothes to make a cowboy."

"Will you show me how to be a cowboy?" asked Danny.

"Yes," said Uncle Mack. "We'll start tomorrow. Why don't you sit down now and write a letter home?" So Danny got out paper and pencil. He sat down at the table and wrote:

Dear Mother and Father:

I am at the ranch. I like it here. Uncle Mack and Aunt Betty gave me cowboy clothes, but I am not a cowboy yet. I am going to start tomorrow.

Your son,
DANNY

III

The Runaway Pony

In the morning Danny ate breakfast with Uncle Mack, Aunt Betty, and six cowboys.

One of the cowboys was called Slim. He had red hair and freckles. He grinned at Danny.

"Guess we're going to have a new cowboy on Bar-K Ranch," he said.

"Yes," said Uncle Mack. "I'm going to teach him to ride today."

After breakfast the cowboys carried their
dishes to the kitchen. Danny carried his dishes
to the kitchen, too. Then the cowboys rode away
to work.

Danny and Uncle Mack went out to the bunk-
house.

"This is where the cowboys sleep," said Uncle Mack.

There were bunk beds along the wall. On the floor were rugs made of the skins of deer, bears, and mountain lions. Saddles, bridles, and ropes hung from pegs on the wall.

Uncle Mack took down a small saddle.

"This will be yours," he said.

They went to the stable. There were horses in some of the stalls. Some of them were eating out of the feedboxes.

"I like this black horse," said Danny.

"His name is Nip," said Uncle Mack. "He is my horse."

"I like this gray horse," said Danny.

"His name is Tuck," said Uncle Mack. "He is your Aunt Betty's horse."

Danny saw a pony. He was white with brown spots.

"I like this spotted pony," he said.

"His name is Ginger," said Uncle Mack. "He is going to be your horse."

Danny rubbed the pony's nose. "You're going to be my horse. I'm going to ride you and feed you and take care of you."

Ginger opened his mouth and made a funny little noise. It sounded like, "Whee-ee!" He rubbed his nose on Danny's hand.

"I know what he wants," said Uncle Mack. "He wants some sugar."

Danny ran to the house. "Aunt Betty, may I have some sugar for Ginger?"

"I'll bring some when I come," said Aunt Betty. "I'm coming out to see you ride."

Danny went back to the stable. Uncle Mack showed him how to put the bridle over Ginger's head and slip the bit into his mouth. He showed him how to saddle Ginger and lead him out of the stable.

"Ginger is a good pony," said Uncle Mack. "He is strong, he can run fast, and he is gentle. Do you want to get on him now?"

Danny put his foot in the stirrup. It was easy to swing himself into the saddle.

"A cowboy sits straight in the saddle," Uncle Mack told him.

"Like this?" asked Danny.

"Yes. Straight, but not stiff. He rides with his legs straight down, and he doesn't bounce around in the saddle."

Aunt Betty came out. She had a white sugar sack in her hand. "There is some sugar in the bottom," she said. "You can give it to the pony."

She held up the sack. The wind was blowing. It took the sack out of her hand and blew it straight into the pony's face.

The pony jumped and ran.

"Whoa!" shouted Danny.

Ginger didn't stop.

Danny pulled on the reins. Ginger kept on running. He was running away.

Down across the pasture he went, as fast as the wind. Danny's hat blew off.

"Whoa!" he shouted.

There were bushes ahead. Danny thought Ginger was going to jump over them. But the pony stopped short. Danny went flying into the air and landed in the bushes.

He lay there a little while. He felt his arms and legs. He wasn't hurt, but he was out of breath.

Uncle Mack came riding up on his black horse. "Danny, are you all right?"

"Yes, I'm all right." Danny rubbed his legs as he came out of the bushes. "I thought you said Ginger was gentle."

"He is," said Uncle Mack, "but when the sugar sack hit him in the face, he didn't know what it was. It made him afraid, so he ran away."

Ginger was standing close to the bushes. Danny went over to him. The pony was not afraid now.

"Do you see why a cowboy wears boots with high heels?" asked Uncle Mack.

Danny shook his head.

"The heels keep his feet from going through the stirrups," said Uncle Mack. "If one of your feet had gone through the stirrup, it might have caught there. You might have been dragged until you were hurt. As it is, you're not hurt at all, are you, Danny?"

"No," said Danny, "but I lost my hat."

"We'll pick it up on the way back," said Uncle Mack.

Danny got on the pony. He and Uncle Mack rode back to the stable together.

"Will I be a cowboy as soon as I learn to ride?" asked Danny.

"A cowboy has to ride," said Uncle Mack, "but he has to do other things, too."

That night Danny wrote another letter.

Dear Mother and Father:

Today I rode a pony. He ran away, I fell off. I was not hurt. I like to ride, but I am not a cowboy yet.

Your son,

DANNY

IV

A Cowboy's Day

"What does a cowboy do all day?" asked Danny.

"I'll ask Slim to take you with him tomorrow," said Uncle Mack. "Then you can see."

In the morning, when Slim rode away, Danny rode with him. They had their raincoats rolled up and tied to their saddles. Inside the raincoats was something to eat. They each had a bacon sandwich and an apple.

"Get up, Ginger," Danny said to his spotted pony.

"Get up, Tony," Slim said to his white horse. "I got my horse from a man named Tony, so I named the horse Tony, too."

Shep, the collie dog, ran out in front of the ranch house and barked.

"He wants to come, too," said Slim.

Shep wagged his tail and came running after them.

While they rode along, the sun came up over the mountains. The day grew warm.

"Where are we going?" asked Danny.

"We are going to drive some cattle to another part of the range where the grass is better," said Slim.

They rode over a hill. At the foot of the hill was a water hole. All around the water hole were white-faced cattle.

"Hey! Hey!" shouted Slim. "Get along!"

The cattle began to move. Slim and Danny drove them across the range.

"Are these all the cattle on the ranch?" asked Danny.

"Oh, no," said Slim. "There are herds in other parts of the ranch. The other cowboys take care of them."

Sometimes a calf tried to run away. Shep was always there to drive it back with the others.

"He's a good cattle dog," said Danny.

"Yes," said Slim. "He knows what to do without being told. We taught him when he was a puppy."

Shep began to bark.

"Look!" said Danny. "He's barking at that little animal up in the rocks."

It was the strangest little animal Danny had ever seen. It looked like a ball with long, sharp stickers standing up all over it.

"That's a porcupine," said Slim. "Those stickers are his quills, and every one is as sharp as a needle. Come away, Shep, or you'll get stuck."

Shep barked a few more times, but he came away.

They came to a spring running out of the rocks. Danny and Slim stopped for a drink of the clear, cold water. They sat down and ate their sandwiches and apples. Then they drove the herd on again.

"Where are we going to take the cattle?" asked Danny.

Slim pointed. "The grass is good at the foot of that mountain. See how green it is? We'll take the cattle there."

"Good," said Danny.

The mountain didn't look far away, but it was nearly dark when they got there.

"This is a good place to leave the cattle for a while," said Slim. "Lots of grass for them to eat. Lots of water coming down the mountain."

"Are we going to ride home now?" asked Danny.

Slim shook his head. "The horses need rest, and so do we. We'll camp here in the cabin to-night."

Danny looked around for the cabin. He saw it back among the pine trees. It was a log cabin with a tin chimney.

"This is one of the cow camps," said Slim. "There are others on the ranch. When a cowboy has to stay all night away from home, he stops at a cow camp."

They tied their horses under the trees and went into the cabin. It was dark inside. Slim lighted an oil lamp.

There was a stove in the cabin. There was a cupboard. There was a wood box full of wood. There were two chairs and a table and two bunks.

"Who keeps the cabin so clean?" asked Danny.

"Every time a cowboy stays here, he leaves the cabin clean and ready for the next man." Slim looked into the cupboard. "We always keep something to eat here. See? Flour, sugar, some cans of milk, and a lot more things. We'll have a good supper tonight."

They had bacon and corn bread for supper. They had corn-meal mush. Slim cooked it in a pan and they ate it with sugar and milk. They

had a can of sweet cherries, too, for their dessert.

"You're a good cook, Slim," said Danny. "Everything tasted good."

"That's because you were hungry." Slim took off his boots. "My bed is going to feel good to-night."

"So is mine," said Danny.

Slim blew out the light and they went to bed.

Just as Danny got to sleep, he woke up.

Outside, a dog was barking and howling.

Slim jumped up. He opened the door wide.

"Here, Shep!" he called. "What's the matter, Shep?"

The dog ran into the cabin.

Slim lighted the lamp. Shep was still howling, and Danny could see why. There were three long stickers in the dog's nose.

"Shep, I'm surprised at you," said Slim. "Don't you know better than to get close to a porcupine?"

He took Shep's head in his hands. He pulled out the sharp stickers. Shep howled with pain, but he was glad to have the stickers pulled out. He licked Slim's hand.

"We'd better keep you inside so you won't get into any more mischief," said Slim.

Shep lay down on the floor with his sore nose between his paws. Slim blew out the light and went back to bed. Danny lay down again. They all slept until morning.

A Cowboy's Life

Give me the range, a po-ny to ride,
Give me a trail through ce-dar and pine,

Give me a dog to run by my side. Just let me wan-der
Give me a herd that I can call mine. Give me a camp-fire

hap-py and free. A cow-boy's life is the life for me!
un-der a tree. A cow-boy's life is the life for me!

Chorus

Sing high on the moun-tain, Sing low on the prai-rie. The west is the coun-try where I want to be. Sing high on the moun-tain sing low on the prai-rie. A cow-boy's life is the life for me!

V

The Lost Calf

In the morning they had an early breakfast.
Then Danny and Slim cleaned the cabin. Slim
cut some wood and Danny filled the wood box.

"Now everything is ready for the next cowboy," said Slim.

They left the cattle eating the good grass at the

foot of the mountain. On the way back to the ranch house they rode faster because they had no cattle to drive.

"Now I know what a cowboy does all day," said Danny.

"A cowboy does other things besides drive cattle," said Slim. "He takes care of his horses. He ropes calves and brands them. Sometimes he shoots a rattlesnake. Sometimes he rides along a fence. If it needs fixing, he fixes it."

"We are riding along a fence now," said Danny.

"Yes, and I see something that needs fixing." Slim got off his horse. He picked up two pieces of broken wire and twisted them together. "If we didn't keep the fences fixed, the cattle would get out and run all over the country."

As they rode toward home, Slim stopped to fix other broken places in the fence.

At one place a tree had fallen over and broken the fence wire.

"This will take longer to fix," said Slim. "Get down and rest if you want to."

Danny got off his pony. There was a rocky hill ahead, and he started to climb it. Shep ran in front of him with his nose close to the ground.

"Shep, are you on the trail of something?" asked Danny.

At the top of the hill the dog stopped. He looked down over the rocks.

Danny thought he had seen another porcupine.

"What is it, Shep?" he asked.

Shep began to bark. Danny climbed up beside him and looked down over the other side of the hill.

At first he saw nothing but rocks, trees, and bushes. Then, far down among the rocks, he saw something move. It was something brown.

Shep was not afraid. Danny was not afraid, either. They started down the hill.

Now Danny could see what was there among the rocks. It was a little brown calf. When Danny and Shep came close, it didn't try to run away.

In a moment Danny saw why. The calf's front foot was caught between two rocks.

Danny tried to lift out the front foot, but he could not move it. He tried to pull the rocks apart, but they were too big for him to move.

He ran up the hill. He called to Slim, "There's a baby calf down here with its foot caught in the rocks."

Slim climbed over the hill. He patted the calf and rubbed its back.

He had the hammer he used to fix the fence. He had a nail in his pocket. He began to drive the nail into the rock close to the calf's foot. A little piece of the rock broke off. He drove the nail in again, and a bigger piece of the rock broke off. In a little while he had broken off so much rock that Danny could move the calf's foot.

"Pull," said Slim.

Danny pulled. The calf's foot came free.

"It's out!" said Danny. "Shall we take it back to the rest of the herd?"

"This is not one of our calves," said Slim.

"It isn't?" said Danny.

"No. All our cattle have the Bar-K brand." Slim pointed to the calf's side. Burned in the calf's hide was the letter *A* with a circle around it. "This calf came from the Circle-A Ranch next to ours. It must have got through the fence where the wire was broken."

The calf could stand, but it could not walk on its front foot.

"Is it hurt?" asked Danny.

Slim ran his hand over the calf's leg. "No bones are broken. I think it was caught in the rocks for so long that the feeling has gone out of its foot."

Slim picked up the brown calf and carried it up the hill.

He asked Danny, "Would you like to take it back to the ranch house while I go on fixing fence?"

"Yes," said Danny, "but how can I take it back?"

"I'll show you," said Slim, "if you'll get on your pony."

Danny got on Ginger. Slim laid the calf in

front of the saddle. Its hind legs hung down on one side, its front legs hung down on the other.

"There," said Slim. "You can carry him like that all the way home."

Danny rode with the calf in front of the saddle. Shep ran beside him.

It was not far to the ranch house. When Danny rode up to the door, Uncle Mack and Aunt Betty came out.

"Oh, the poor little calf!" said Aunt Betty. "What's the matter with it?"

"Its foot was caught in the rocks," said Danny. "It isn't hurt, but it can't walk yet."

Uncle Mack saw the brand on the calf's side. "This is a Circle-A calf. Would you like to take it back where it belongs?"

"Yes, I would," said Danny.

"Just go down the road until you come to the first house," said Uncle Mack. "That is the Circle-A ranch house."

Danny rode along. He came to a big yellow house with a green roof. He rode up to it.

Dogs barked, and a boy came out of the house. He was almost as big as Danny. He was dressed like Danny, too, in blue jeans and a checkered shirt.

"Where did you find Trixie!" he shouted. He ran out and put his arms around the calf. "Where have you been, Trixie? I've looked everywhere for you!"

"We found her on our ranch," said Danny. "Her foot was caught in the rocks."

"Trixie is my pet calf," said the boy. "I was afraid I would never find her again."

Danny got down and helped him lift Trixie off the horse. The feeling had come back into the calf's foot. She took a few steps. She began to run and play. Before long she was cutting circles all over the yard. The boy laughed. "Trixie always plays like that. Isn't she funny?"

"Yes," said Danny. "I wish I had a calf like Trixie."

"I have a dog, too, and a pet lamb, and some kittens," said the boy. "Come out to the barn if you'd like to see them."

On the way to the barn the boy told Danny his name was Jerry Bell. "This is my father's ranch."

"My name is Danny Hopper," said Danny. "I live on the Bar-K Ranch."

"That makes us neighbors," said Jerry. "I want you to come to see me again."

"I will," said Danny, "and I wish you would come to see me."

That night he wrote to Mother and Father:

Slim and I stayed at the cow camp last night. On the way home we found a calf from the Circle-A Ranch. I took her home. She was Jerry Bell's calf. Jerry and I are going to play together. I like it here and wish you were here, too. Some day I am going to be a cowboy.

Your son,
DANNY

VI

Chipper

Every morning when Danny woke up, the first thing he saw from his window was the flat-topped mountain. Sometimes he lay there looking at it. It looked as flat as a floor. He wondered what was on top of it.

"Some day," he said to himself, "I'm going up there."

One morning his chance came.

45

Uncle Mack said, "I'm going to see a man about buying some cattle. He lives on the flat-topped mountain. Would you like to go with me?"

"Yes, I would," said Danny.

"Would Jerry like to go, too?" asked Uncle Mack.

"Let's stop at his house, and I'll ask him," said Danny.

They stopped at Jerry's house.

"Yes," said Jerry. "I want to go."

So the three of them rode away in Uncle Mack's car.

Danny asked Jerry, "Have you ever been on the flat-topped mountain?"

"Lots of times," said Jerry.

"Is it as flat as it looks?" asked Danny.

Jerry and Uncle Mack began to laugh.

"Danny is going to be surprised, isn't he?" said Uncle Mack.

"Yes, he is," said Jerry.

They drove up the mountain road. When they came to the top, Danny looked all around.

"It isn't flat at all!" he said.

"No," said Uncle Mack. "It only looks flat when you see it from below."

There were hills and valleys on top of the mountain. There were trees and pastures. There were streams and lakes, and Danny saw islands out in the lakes.

Uncle Mack found the man he had come to see. His name was Mr. Ridd. He lived by a lake.

While the men sat by the lake and talked, Danny and Jerry went swimming. The water was so clear they could see all the way to the bottom. At first it was cold, but after they had been in it a little while, it felt warm.

When they were tired of swimming, the men took them fishing. They went in Mr. Ridd's boat. They all caught some fish.

"I've got a bite," Jerry would say, and pull a fish into the boat.

At the same time, Danny would say, *"I've* got a bite!" and pull in another fish.

They made a fire by the lake. They cooked the fish and ate them all.

"I'm still hungry!" said Danny.

"So am I," said Jerry.

"I'll get you some peanuts," said Uncle Mack. "Will that do until we get home?"

They said good-by to Mr. Ridd and started back to the ranch. When they came to a store, Uncle Mack bought a big sack of peanuts. Danny and Jerry ate them while they rode along.

Just before they started down the mountain, Uncle Mack stopped the car. "If you look here," he said, "you may see some chipmunks."

"I see one!" said Jerry.

"Where?" asked Danny. "Oh, I see one too!"

The boys jumped out of the car. Chipmunks were playing around an old stump.

"They look like little gray squirrels," said Danny.

"Only they have stripes down their backs," said Jerry.

"I wish I had one for a pet," said Danny. "Look at this one. See him hold out his paws."

"He wants something to eat," said Unc

Mack. "Are there any peanuts left in that sack?"

There was one peanut left.

Danny sat down by the stump and held out the peanut. The chipmunk came close. He shook his tail and ran away. He came close again.

Danny sat very still. He held the peanut out in his hand. The chipmunk came close and held out his paws. Just as he reached for the peanut, Danny reached for him.

He caught him around the middle. The chip-

munk squealed. Danny popped him into the sack.

"I caught him! I caught him!" he cried.

"Are you going to keep him?" asked Jerry.

"Yes," said Danny.

"Are you sure you want to keep him?" asked Uncle Mack. "You'll have to take care of him, you know."

"I'll take care of him," said Danny. "I'll make a pet of him."

He took the chipmunk back to the ranch. He made a cage out of a box. He put the chipmunk into it.

"I'm going to call you Chipper," he said.

Every day he brought Chipper food and water. He gave him dry grass for a bed.

But Chipper didn't make a bed. He ate and drank only a little. All day he sat and looked out of the cage.

Danny tried to pet him. But when he put his hand into the cage, Chipper hid in the grass.

Danny kept the cage on the back porch. Slim came by and looked at Chipper.

"That's a sad chipmunk," he said.

"I've been good to him," said Danny. "Why is he sad?"

"Don't you know?" asked Slim.

"No, Slim, I don't," said Danny.

"He used to live on the mountain," said Slim.

"His home was up there. He used to run in the sun and wind, and he played with the other chipmunks. How do you think he feels down here, shut up in a box?"

Danny looked at Chipper. "I wanted him to be my pet."

"A baby chipmunk might grow up here and like to be a pet," said Slim, "but Chipper is a grown-up chipmunk. He can't forget he used to be free."

Danny gave the chipmunk some fresh water and grass and leaves.

"Eat your dinner, Chipper," he said.

But Chipper wouldn't eat.

Danny went to Uncle Mack. "When are you going back to the flat-topped mountain?" he asked.

"I'm going back tomorrow," said Uncle Mack.

"I want to go with you," said Danny.

The next morning they drove away. Danny had Chipper's cage on his knee.

They came to the top of the mountain. "There is the stump where I caught Chipper," said Danny. "Will you stop here, please?"

Uncle Mack stopped the car. Danny got out and set the cage on the stump. He opened the door. "There, Chipper," he said. "I brought you back."

The chipmunk sat up. He turned his nose to the wind. He shook his tail.

"Go on," said Danny.

Chipper jumped out of the cage. He sat on his hind legs. He ran up over the rocks as if he were flying. "Good-by, Chipper," said Danny.

He got back into the car.

"Look," said Uncle Mack, as they drove away.

Chipper was sitting high on a rock. He was chattering and shaking his paws.

"He's saying good-by," said Uncle Mack. "Maybe he's saying, 'Thank you for bringing me home.' "

VII

Fire in the Grass

Danny and Jerry were riding their ponies across the range. Danny was taking salt to the cattle. Jerry had come along to help carry the salt.

Danny had two big blocks of salt in a sack tied to his saddle. Jerry had two more blocks on *his* saddle.

The sun beat down on their heads.

"It's hot, isn't it?" said Danny.

"Yes," said Jerry. "This has been a hot, dry summer. See how dry the grass is getting."

"The cattle eat it, even if it *is* dry," said Danny.

They rode to the water hole where the cattle were eating and drinking. They set the salt on the grass near the water hole. The cattle came to lick the smooth, white blocks.

"Salt must be like candy to them," said Jerry.

Danny went up to a cow in the herd. She had a white face and a dark ring around one eye. He patted her back. "Hello, Wander," he said.

"'Wander,'" said Jerry. "That's a funny name."

"Slim calls her Wander because she likes to wander off by herself," said Danny. "She has twin calves. See them playing together?"

"She watches them all the time," said Jerry.

"Yes," said Danny. "Wander takes good care of her twins."

"Has your uncle ever given you a calf of your own?" asked Jerry.

"No," said Danny, "because I won't be here much longer."

"Why not?" asked Jerry.

"I have to go back to the city," said Danny. "I have to be there when school starts."

"Won't you be here for the fall roundup?" asked Jerry.

Danny shook his head.

"Oh, that's too bad," said Jerry. "I like round-up time best of all. The cowboys drive all the herds together. They find the calves that haven't been branded and they rope and brand them. Some of the cattle go into the feeding pens and some are sold and some go back to the range. I wish you could see how the cowboys and horses and dogs all know how to work together."

"I wish I could, too," said Danny.

"And after that they have a rodeo in town," said Jerry. "All the best riders are there. They rope calves and ride wild horses. There are cow-girls, too, and the band plays. It's the best show you ever saw."

"Maybe I can see a roundup and a rodeo some day," said Danny.

He and Jerry rode back toward the ranch house. On the way they came to Indian Rock. It was a high rock standing alone on the range.

Danny and Jerry got off their ponies and

looked at it. "There's paint on it," said Danny. "I see red paint and yellow paint."

"That's Indian writing," Jerry told him, "but no one knows what it means."

"Uncle Mack told me the Indians lived here a long time ago," said Danny.

"My father says this rock was their lookout," said Jerry. "They climbed up here to look for buffalo and deer."

"Or maybe to look for other Indians," said Danny. "Let's go to the top and see what we can see."

He began to climb. Jerry climbed right behind him.

"It looks as if steps have been cut in the rock," said Danny.

"Maybe the Indians did cut steps," said Jerry.

Danny came to the top. He turned and helped Jerry up. They both stood on top of Indian Rock.

"You can see a long way," said Jerry.

"Yes, you can," said Danny. "I see the cattle."

"I see the ranch house," said Jerry.

"I see the creek and the road," said Danny. "I see where the road goes into the woods."

They looked for a while. Then Jerry started down.

"Wait," said Danny. "I see something else."

It was a puff of white near the road.

"It looks like a little cloud," said Jerry.

"Jerry, it's smoke!" cried Danny. "It's a grass fire!"

Uncle Mack had told him how bad grass fires could be. Sometimes they started when someone threw down a lighted match or forgot to put out a campfire.

"It could burn the whole ranch!" said Jerry.

He and Danny slid down the rock.

"Ride to the house, Jerry," said Danny, "and get somebody to help. I'll go to the fire and try to put it out."

Jerry rode off. Danny rode toward the fire as fast as Ginger could go.

Now he could see the fire. He could hear it crackle in the grass.

Ginger snorted when he smelled the smoke.

Danny jumped off. He pulled the blanket out from under the saddle.

"Go home, Ginger," he said. "You can't help me here."

He ran to the creek and dipped the blanket into the water.

There was a wide, black spot where the grass had burned. The wind was blowing the fire toward the woods.

Danny stood between the fire and the woods. He beat the fire with the wet blanket. Sparks flew up around him. The smoke hurt his eyes.

He was putting out some of the fire, but it was getting closer and closer to the woods.

Someone called his name.

He saw a man coming toward him through the smoke. It was Uncle Mack!

Slim and Jerry were there, too. So were some of the men from Circle-A Ranch.

They all worked together. They poured water on the fire. They beat it out with wet sacks and blankets.

Soon the fire was nearly out. There were only a few sparks left, and the cowboys were stamping them out with their boots.

"Danny kept the fire out of the woods," said Jerry.

"Yes," said Uncle Mack. "If it hadn't been for Danny, we might have had something worse than a grass fire. We might have had a forest fire."

"Did Ginger get to the stable?" asked Danny.

"Yes," said Uncle Mack, "but you can ride home with me." So they all went back to the ranch house. Fighting the fire had made them thirsty. They were so thirsty they drank a bucket of lemonade and a bucket of water, besides.

That night Danny wrote a letter:

Dear Mother and Father:

   We had a grass fire. I helped put it out. Uncle Mack says I may be a fireman instead of a cowboy. But I would rather be a cowboy.

Your son,
DANNY

VIII

The Canyon Trail

Danny and Slim were riding the range near the mountains. They came to the cow camp.

"Look at that herd of white-faced cattle out in the sun," said Slim. "Isn't that a pretty sight?"

It *was* a pretty sight. Most of the cattle were eating grass. Some were lying down. Some of the calves were playing, running in and out of the herd.

Slim and Danny rode among them to make sure they were all right.

"I don't see Wander and her twin calves," said Danny.

"I guess she wandered off again," said Slim. "It's bad when they wander too far from the herd. There are wolves in the mountains. When they find a cow alone, they run after her and pull her down. A cow will fight, but she hasn't much chance against a wolf."

"I hope they don't catch Wander and her twins," said Danny.

"Maybe they are over here in the trees," said Slim. "I'll ride this way. You ride that way. If I find them first, I'll call you."

"And if I find them first, I'll call you," said Danny.

He rode until he came to the fence. He came to a place where a fence post had broken. The wire was down. He thought he saw tracks where

cattle had walked across it, but he was not sure.

"Get up, Ginger," he said. The pony walked over the wire.

There was a spring ahead. The water had made a pool. In the mud by the pool, Danny saw tracks. He saw that a cow and two calves had stopped here to drink.

"Come on, Ginger," he said. "Wander and her twins were here. We'll find them and drive them back."

As he rode slowly along, he found more tracks.

There was a canyon ahead. The rocks were steep and high on both sides. Wander's tracks led into the canyon.

He thought he saw her ahead.

"Hey!" he shouted.

But it was only a rock.

He rode up the canyon. There were two trails. He saw Wander's tracks on one of them and he knew that this was the one to take.

The trail ran up and down, between trees and over rocks. Around every bend he looked for Wander and the twins.

At last he saw them. The calves were under a tree. Wander was eating leaves from the tree.

"What a cow!" said Danny. "With all the good grass on the range, you have to wander down the canyon and eat leaves off a tree!"

He tried to drive her back, but Wander didn't want to go. She tried to run away.

Ginger was a good cattle pony. He ran in front of her and drove her back.

"Now," said Danny, "back to the range you go."

All at once he saw that it was getting dark. Night came early in the canyon. The canyon walls shut out the sun.

He tried to make the cow and calves go faster, but Wander wanted to stop and eat leaves and the calves wanted to play.

"Hey!" shouted Danny. "Move along, move

along. We've got to get out of here before dark."

But it was nearly dark already. Danny could not see the trail. Ginger ran into a tree.

"I never saw that tree before," said Danny. "Maybe I got off the trail."

He called, "Hi! Slim!"

There was no answer. Only his echo came back to him. *"Hi! Slim!"*

It was dark now.

Danny said to Ginger, "We'll have to camp here tonight. In the morning we can find our way out."

He tied the pony to a bush. He felt on the ground for sticks and dry wood and started a fire.

"Come on, Wander," he said. "Don't you wander off again."

He took the rope off his saddle and made a halter around her head as he had seen Slim do, and tied her to a tree. Then he sat down by the fire to wait until morning.

IX

Night

Danny made a bed of pine needles. He lay down and tried to sleep. There were strange sounds in the night. Owls were crying. There was a sound like someone whispering. That was the wind in the pine trees. A long way off an animal was howling. Danny didn't know whether it was a dog or a wolf.

Ginger was not asleep. He was shaking his

head. The cow was not asleep. She was standing under the trees. The calves were close to her. They all seemed to be afraid.

Danny put more wood on the fire. When the sparks flew up, he saw something move out in the night. It looked like a big, gray dog, and it moved without a sound. It was a wolf.

Danny picked up a rock. He threw it as hard as he could.

For a long time the wolf didn't come back. Then Danny saw it again. Its yellow eyes were shining.

Danny threw more rocks. He threw all he could find.

But the wolf kept coming back. Danny saw its yellow eyes.

He had no more rocks to throw. He shouted to drive the wolf back.

At first it stayed away, but after a while it was not afraid when Danny shouted. It came closer.

Danny had a new idea. He took a burning stick out of the fire and threw it. The wolf howled. Then it ran.

He made a bigger fire. All night he kept it burning, and he threw burning sticks to keep the wolf back.

Daylight began to come over the canyon walls. Danny was so tired he could hardly walk, but he could rest now. The wolf had gone back up the canyon.

He started to put out the fire.

Ginger turned his head. His ears stood up.

"What's the matter?" said Danny. "Did you hear something?"

He listened. Something was moving in the canyon not far away.

Someone shouted, "Danny!"

He forgot he was sleepy and tired. He jumped up and ran down the canyon. Just around the bend he met Slim!

Slim was riding his horse.

"Danny! Where have you been?"

"Here in the canyon," said Danny.

"I looked for you all night," said Slim. "When the sun came up, I tracked you into the canyon."

"I found Wander and the calves," said Danny, "but it got dark before I could find my way out of the canyon."

Danny led the way to Ginger and Wander and the calves.

"What's this?" said Slim. "Look at those wolf tracks!"

"Yes," said Danny. "A wolf came to eat Wander and the calves. I threw rocks and burning sticks to keep it away."

"And you stayed here all night and kept the wolf away?" said Slim. "Danny, this makes you a real cowboy."

"Why?" asked Danny.

"Above everything else, a cowboy takes care of his cattle. Last night you took care of *your* cattle, and no cowboy could have done better."

"And I'm a real cowboy?" asked Danny.

"You're a real cowboy," said Slim. "No one can say you're not."

"That's what I've always wanted to be," said Danny. "Wait until I write and tell Mother and Father!"

Slim smiled as if he knew a secret. But Danny didn't see him smiling.

X

Surprise for Danny

It was afternoon, and Danny sat in his room. He was sleepy and tired. Uncle Mack and Aunt Betty had told him to go to bed. In a little while he was going, but first he wanted to write his mother and father about what had happened last night.

He got out his pencil and paper and wrote:

Dear Mother and Father:

   Now I am a cowboy. Slim said so and Uncle Mack said so. I was in the canyon all night with Wander and her twin calves. I kept the wolf away. Uncle Mack is going to give me the twin calves, and some day—

That was as far as he got. He was too sleepy to sit up. The pencil fell out of his hand. He put his head down on the table. He was asleep.

   An hour later he was still asleep when the door opened. A woman came in. Then a man came in. A cat came in behind them.

   "Look, he's asleep," said the woman.

   "He was writing a letter," said the man.

   The woman said, "Danny!"

   Danny sat up. He looked and rubbed his eyes. He looked again.

"Mother — Father!" he cried.

"Danny!" they cried. "How is our cowboy?"

They made so much noise that Jill, the cat, ran and hid under the bed.

"I didn't know you were coming," said Danny. "Why didn't someone tell me?"

"Your Uncle Mack and Aunt Betty knew," said Mother, "but we knew you liked surprises, so we wanted to give you one."

"I was just writing you a letter," said Danny. "I wanted to tell you about last night. I was in the canyon with Wander and her twin calves and the wolf came—"

"We know," said Father. "Everyone on the ranch is talking about it."

"That was a brave thing to do," said Mother.

"And Uncle Mack is going to give me the twin calves for my own," said Danny. "I want you to see them. I want you to see Ginger, too. Let's go see them now."

"Wait," said Mother. "We have lots of time." She asked Father, "Shall we tell him now?"

"Yes, let's tell him," Father said. "We saved the biggest surprise for the last. Danny, we read your letters about how you liked the ranch and wished we were here. I used to be a cowboy, you

know, and ever since I left the West, I've wanted
to come back, so—"

"You're going to stay?" cried Danny. "You and
Mother are going to stay for good?"

"Yes, for good," said Mother. "We'll stay here
for a while. Some day we hope to have a ranch of
our own not far away."

"We're all going to stay!" shouted Danny.

"We'll all be here for the roundup, and we'll see the rodeo, too. Come on, let's tell Slim. Let's find Jerry and tell him. Let's tell *everybody!*"

They started out to the stable. Danny led the way.

"There goes our cowboy," said Mother.

"He may not be the biggest cowboy in the West," said Father, "but he must be the happiest one!"

I'll Meet You at the Roundup

I'll meet you at the round-up in the fall.— It's

round-up time I like the best of all.— When the herds come in from

ev'ry-where, Look a-round for me and I'll be there At the round - up, the

round up I'll meet you at the round-up in the fall.—